ROYAL RESCUES

The Lost Puppy

Paula Harrison

illustrated by Olivia Chin Mueller

Feiwel and Friends • New York

To Scooby, the best dog in the world

A Feiwel and Friends Book
An imprint of Macmillan Publishing Group, LLC
120 Broadway, New York, NY 10271

Royal Rescues: The Lost Puppy. Text copyright © 2019
by Paula Harrison. Illustrations copyright © 2019 by Olivia Chin Mueller.
All rights reserved. Printed in the United States of America by LSC
Communications, Crawfordsville, Indiana.

Our books may be purchased in bulk for promotional, educational, or business
use. Please contact your local bookseller or the Macmillan Corporate and
Premium Sales Department at (800) 221-7945 ext. 5442 or by email at
MacmillanSpecialMarkets@macmillan.com.

Library of Congress Cataloging-in-Publication Data is available.

ISBN 978-1-250-26490-9 (hardcover)
1 3 5 7 9 10 8 6 4 2

ISBN 978-1-250-25925-7 (trade paperback)
5 7 9 10 8 6 4

ISBN 978-1-250-25926-4 (ebook)

Book design by Nosy Crow
Feiwel and Friends logo designed by Filomena Tuosto

First published in the UK by Nosy Crow as
Princess of Pets: The Lost Puppy in 2019.
mackids.com

Chapter One
Bea's
Secret Pets

Bea was woken as usual by a tiny rustling under her bed. Kneeling down, she reached for the cardboard box hidden underneath and carefully lifted the lid. A pink, whiskery nose poked out of the straw inside, and two black eyes peeped up at her.

"Morning, Fluff!" Bea smiled at the little mouse. "Shall I fetch you some more cereal for breakfast?"

The little mouse scrambled out of the hay and ran around and around in circles.

Bea laughed. "You must be hungry." She heard a creak outside the bedroom door. "Back soon!" she whispered, pushing the box under the bed and jumping to her feet.

The door swung open, and her older sister stomped into the bedroom. Natasha was wearing a blue satin dress, and her hair was perfectly smooth and neat. "It's late!" she snapped. "You should have been up ages ago." She pulled open the curtains, and sunlight poured in.

Bea glanced out the window. The truck that brought hay for the horses was driving away from the royal stables. A cloud of seagulls swooped and wheeled in the sky. Beyond the palace wall there was a glimpse of the sea, glittering like blue treasure.

Bea shrugged. It was annoying when Natasha acted as if she was in charge. "It can't be that late. Anyway, I *am* up!"

Nine-year-old Bea (which was short for Beatrice) was the middle child of the three royal children. They lived at Ruby Palace with their father, King George, and all the royal servants. Their mother had died from a fever when their brother, Alfie, was little.

"You'd better hurry up, Bea!" Natasha's frown deepened. "You know breakfast is at eight o'clock."

"I'll come down in a minute." Bea hesitated. Had she put the lid back on Fluff's box properly? She sneakily tried to feel under the bed with her foot.

"What are you doing?" asked Natasha. But before Bea could answer, a small boy in red pajamas burst through the door.

"I dreamed I rode a dinosaur!" said Alfie. "A T-Rex with giant teeth. Did you know the largest T-Rex tooth ever found was almost a foot long?"

Natasha sighed. "You're not dressed, either! Well, I'm not waiting for you two." She marched away down the corridor, and Alfie dashed after her.

Bea shut the door and knelt down by the bed again. "Sorry, Fluff!" She settled the lid of the mouse's box into place. "I didn't mean to scare you."

Bea was mad about animals, and her bedroom walls were covered with cute animal posters and pictures that she'd cut out of magazines. She'd spent months and months asking her dad to get her a pet. But after begging in vain for hamsters, guinea pigs, and even a goldfish, Bea began to despair. King George's reply was always the same: *Beatrice, the royal palace is no place for a pet.*

Since then she'd begun secretly looking after any animal that needed a home. It had started with Crinkly, the spider she'd found in the royal kitchen. Bea had saved him from Mrs. Stickler, the royal housekeeper, and found him a home in her bedroom drawer. Then she'd taken Fluff from a lonely hole behind the piano in the dining room.

Her biggest rescue so far was saving a little kitten who'd gotten stuck in a tree. Tiger now slept in the laundry room and played in the palace stables during the day.

After pulling on jeans and a yellow T-shirt, Bea hurried to breakfast. Halfway down the stairs, she heard feet thudding behind her.

"Race you!" cried Alfie, dashing past.

Bea rushed after her brother, overtaking him as she reached the last step. "I won!" she gasped, flinging herself through the dining room doorway.

"No, you didn't!" Alfie grabbed her arm.

Suddenly Bea realized that her father was sitting at the dining table, looking very annoyed. This was bad luck! The king was normally hard at work on royal business by now. She skidded to a halt,

her heart thumping. Alfie ran straight
into her, and they tumbled to the floor in
a tangle of arms and legs.

"Beatrice! Alfred! I expect you to
arrive for a meal in a graceful manner."
King George frowned, his thick eyebrows
squeezing together. "Beatrice, you're
older and you should be setting your
brother a good example."

"Sorry!" Bea tried to sit down at the
table gracefully.

Mrs. Stickler brought in a tray of
boiled eggs and toast. She set the tray on
the table and poured apple juice into
three crystal glasses.

"Children, I have something
important to tell you . . . ," began the
king. "Lord and Lady Villiers are coming
to dinner this evening, so you must be
on your very best behavior. They want

to find somewhere to live along the cliff top—somewhere with a nice view."

Bea looked up. The cliff top above Savara was where her best friend, Keira, lived. Her parents ran the Sleepy Gull Café, which served the best spring rolls in Savara. Bea often went there to play.

"Natasha and Beatrice—I'd like you to sing the Neravian national song for our guests," continued the king. "Please practice it today so you're note-perfect."

Mrs. Stickler coughed. "Their best clothes have become a little worn, sire, so perhaps I should fetch the dressmaker. With Mr. Wells away, there's plenty of time for clothes fittings."

Bea's heart sank. Mr. Wells, their royal teacher, was on vacation, which meant there were no lessons. She'd hoped to spend the morning playing with Tiger in the stables, not having dress fittings.

"Thank you, Mrs. Stickler." The king straightened his crown. "Perhaps you can help the prince and princesses with their deportment, too. Beatrice and Alfred need to practice proper royal manners."

"Deportment! What's that?" asked Bea.

Natasha looked smug. "It's how to act like a princess, silly! You learn how to walk elegantly and that kind of thing."

Bea sighed. She didn't want to be elegant. She just wanted to spend more time with her pets. Sneakily, she gathered a handful of breakfast cereal and hid it down her sock, ready to give to Fluff.

"I'd be happy to help, sire." Mrs. Stickler turned to the children. "Come to the parlor in half an hour, please."

Suddenly Bea heard the faint sound of barking. She looked out the window eagerly. Was there a dog outside the palace wall?

The housekeeper bustled out of the room and the king left, too, muttering about all the royal business he needed to attend to. The barking came again, ending in a sad whine. Bea listened hard. It sounded as if the dog might be hurt.

Alfie stopped halfway through dipping toast into his boiled egg. "Did you hear that?"

Bea frowned at her brother and gave a tiny shake of her head. She was desperate to get outside and look for the animal, but she didn't want Natasha guessing where she'd gone. "Yes, it sounds really windy out there. I heard the wind blowing, too."

"No, I heard a—" Alfie gasped as Bea kicked him under the table.

Natasha got up and smoothed her dress. "You're so silly, Bea! I can't believe you didn't know what deportment is."

Bea made a face as Natasha left. Then she rushed to the window. "That bark sounded really close. I'm going to see what kind of dog it is. Don't tell Natasha!"

Opening the window wide, Bea climbed onto the sill, swung her legs out,

and slid into the flower bed below. She often went outside this way. It meant she didn't have to pass Mrs. Stickler or anyone else who thought she should be sitting still and keeping her clothes neat instead of running around in the garden.

Bea yanked her jeans free from a thorn and stopped to listen. A gust of wind lifted her wavy hair. The sun beamed down on a tiny lizard that was warming itself on the path. The palace's round golden towers stretched into the bright blue sky.

This time instead of a bark there was a long whimper. Bea's heart thumped as she ran to the palace wall. The dog definitely sounded sad . . . but where was it?

She used the footholds between the bricks to clamber up the wall. A blast of salty air hit her as she reached the top. Out in Savara Harbor the boats were sailing in with their catches of fish, and seagulls whirled overhead.

Bea peered at the road just beyond the wall. There was no sign of a dog. Could it be hidden among the bushes?

The whining came again, and Bea froze. The sound wasn't outside the wall. That meant the dog must be somewhere in the palace garden!

Chapter Two

Big Brown Eyes and Floppy Ears

Bea looked around the garden, wondering where the dog could be. Nothing was moving in the orchard among the plum trees and lemon trees. She listened again, but all she could hear were seagulls calling and the distant whinny of a horse in the royal stables.

Maybe the little dog was in the royal maze or the herb garden! Bea dashed through the archway into the herb

garden and peered under the bench.
Then she hurried into the orchard and
searched among the plum trees. Why
did the palace garden have to be so
enormous? There were thousands of
places a dog could be hiding.

"Hey, puppy!" she called softly.
"Where are you?"

She'd reached the stables when she
heard the whining again, and this time
it was much fainter. She must be going
in the wrong direction. Bea spun around
and headed back to the orchard.

The whimpering noise led her into the
herb garden again. Bea frowned. How
could the little dog sound so close when
she couldn't see it? She looked behind
the clumps of thyme and rosemary.
Then she remembered the fountain and
leaned over the stone ledge to look inside.

Staring up at her was a gorgeous puppy with big brown eyes and floppy ears.

Its fur was a mixture of white and soft blue-gray.

"You're lovely, aren't you?" said Bea. "What are you doing in there?"

The dog trembled and backed away a little. Bea noticed the tiny puddle of water at the bottom of the basin. The fountain was only turned on in the summer, but a pool of rainwater must have collected inside. Maybe the poor thing had jumped in because it was thirsty, and then the steep sides of the fountain had stopped it from getting out again.

Bea clambered onto the edge of the fountain. "Don't worry! I'll help you."

The puppy shivered and gave a little whine. Bea let the little dog sniff her fingers. She wished she had some food the puppy might like. The cereal she'd stuffed down her sock for Fluff wouldn't be any good.

Suddenly she felt something warm and rough on her hand. The little dog had licked her! "We must be friends, then!" Bea knelt down, ignoring the puddle of water soaking into her jeans. Gently, she stroked the puppy's white-and-gray coat, which smelled of herbs like the flower beds below. "I wonder where you came from. You definitely shouldn't be here all by yourself."

She scrambled out of the fountain and lifted the puppy into her arms. Scraps of hay were stuck to the dog's back, so she brushed them off. "You poor thing! You're covered in hay and you're wet, too."

Mrs. Cherry, the palace gardener, was passing the orchard with one of the grooms. Bea trusted Mrs. Cherry. The gardener understood how much Bea loved animals and hadn't minded at all when she'd made a home for a family of doves in the garden shed a few weeks ago. Cuddling the puppy, Bea went to meet them.

"Hello, Princess Bea. What a lovely dog!" said Mrs. Cherry, examining the puppy. "Is she yours?"

"No, I've just found her," explained Bea. "Do you know if anyone's lost a puppy?"

The groom shook his head, and Mrs. Cherry looked puzzled. "I haven't seen anyone looking for a dog, but I can ask around for you."

"Thank you." Bea carried the puppy toward the palace. She wanted to get inside, dry the little dog, and find her something to eat. The puppy needed to be properly looked after until her owner was found.

Creeping up to the back door, she peered through the kitchen window.

Darou, the royal chef, was singing at the top of his lungs while he chopped an onion. Bea knew that if the chef saw an animal in his kitchen, he was sure to make a big fuss and call the guards. She stepped back from the window as Mrs. Stickler walked into the room. When she peeked again, the housekeeper and the cook had disappeared into the pantry. This could be her chance!

Slipping through the back door, she went straight to the fridge. What did dogs like to eat? She rummaged through the shelves, and the puppy leaned forward to sniff at some chicken slices. "Is that what you'd like?" Bea whispered.

A snatch of conversation drifted out of the pantry: ". . . really have to think of something better than mushroom stew. These are important guests, you know."

"I decide the menu! No one else will decide."

Bea grinned. Chef Darou could get very stressed at times. He was also known for storming off, so she needed to be quick. She grabbed the wrapped-up chicken slices and stuffed them into her pocket. The puppy gave a hungry whine.

"It's all right! These are for you," murmured Bea, running out of the kitchen.

Halfway up the stairs, she heard footsteps at the top and spotted her sister's dress through the banister. She twisted around, heart racing. She had to find somewhere to hide the puppy. Natasha was bound to say it was against royal rules to bring a dog inside before going straight to tell Mrs. Stickler.

The sound of voices came from the kitchen. Bea hesitated. She was trapped—she couldn't reach the back door or get upstairs. Dashing into the laundry room, she closed the door, placed the puppy in an empty laundry basket, and hid the basket behind a pile of sheets.

There was no sign of Tiger, who slept in there at night. The kitten was probably playing near the stables. Bea suddenly wondered whether Tiger and the little dog would like each other. She'd just given the puppy the chicken slices when the door burst open.

"What are you doing?" Natasha stuck her hands on her hips.

Bea jumped. "Nothing! I mean . . . I was just checking if my favorite dress had been washed."

Natasha frowned. "You don't have a favorite dress. You wear jeans most of the time."

"I do have a favorite! It's that blue one with the stars on the front." Bea coughed to hide the sound of chomping as the puppy ate a slice of chicken. Then she pretended to look through a pile of laundry. "Anyway, it isn't here, so—"

"You're late," Natasha interrupted. "The dressmaker needs to measure you."

"I'm coming." Bea stepped outside and shut the door quickly. Hopefully the puppy would be all right in the laundry basket for a few minutes.

She followed her sister reluctantly to the parlor. Mr. Jennings, a small man with silver spectacles, was waiting there with a tape measure. Alfie was sitting on the sofa, looking bored.

"Sorry, Mr. Jennings," began Bea.

"There you are, Princess Beatrice!" Mrs. Stickler marched in behind them and eyed Bea disapprovingly. "Please stand still to be measured. I'm sure you don't want to keep Mr. Jennings waiting even more than you have already."

Bea stood still while the dressmaker measured around her waist. She brushed white dog hairs off her sleeve, hoping Mr. Jennings wouldn't notice.

Mr. Jennings folded up his tape measure. "I have everything I need," he told the housekeeper. "We'll get to work on these outfits immediately."

"Thank you, Mr. Jennings," said Mrs. Stickler. "I'll see you again this afternoon. All right, prince and princesses. Let me teach you all about deportment."

Bea stared at the housekeeper in horror. She'd totally forgotten about the lesson in acting elegant. She couldn't leave the puppy alone any longer. What if someone found her? What if she chewed the sheets in the laundry basket to bits? She had to get back to the little dog right away!

Chapter Three
Mrs. Stickler's Deportment Training

Mrs. Stickler handed a book each to Bea, Natasha, and Alfie. "The first thing you need to learn is how to walk gracefully. No one wants to see you plodding into dinner tonight like a cart horse."

"Or a stegosaurus." Alfie grinned. "Or maybe a brachiosaurus. They're huge!"

Bea turned her book over to look at the title. "Why do I need to read *Ships from Olden Days*, Mrs. Stickler?"

The housekeeper sighed. "You're not reading it, Princess Beatrice. You're placing it on your head."

Bea stared. Was Mrs. Stickler joking?

"It makes you stand up straight when you walk." Natasha placed her own book on her head. "I bet I can do it—easy!" She took dainty little steps, crossing the room with the book perfectly balanced.

"Well done!" The housekeeper beamed at Natasha. "Now it's your turn, Princess Beatrice."

Bea put the book on her head and it wobbled. She managed a few steps, but halfway across the room she heard a whining noise outside the door. It sounded just like the puppy, but how had the little animal gotten out of the laundry room?

She strained to listen and suddenly realized that Natasha, Alfie, and Mrs. Stickler were all staring at her. She tripped over a chair, and the book went flying.

"Princess Beatrice! I really hope you don't do *that* this evening." Mrs. Stickler frowned. "Alfie, perhaps you'd better have a turn."

"I don't want to do it!" huffed Alfie. "This book is too heavy."

Mrs. Stickler sighed. "Let me find you another one."

Bea heard a faint scratching outside, and she was sure it was the puppy. She longed to open the door and hug the little dog, but then Mrs. Stickler would throw the poor animal out of the palace forever.

Bea edged over to Alfie and whispered in his ear, "Hey, I need your help."

"Why?" Alfie looked puzzled.

"There's a puppy outside the door," said Bea.

Alfie's eyes widened. "Why is there a puppy—" he began loudly.

"Shh!" Bea nudged him. "I'll explain later! Just try to distract them. Tell them you've hurt yourself or something. But make it big. I've got to catch the dog without them seeing."

"Okay!" Alfie nodded, his face solemn.

"Here you are, Prince Alfred." The housekeeper handed Alfie a smaller book.

"Thank you." Alfie put the book on his head and tottered unsteadily to the middle of the room. "Wow, all this book-balancing makes me feel *really* dizzy!" He rocked from side to side, faking a shocked expression.

"Don't be silly, Alfie!" said Natasha. "*I* don't feel dizzy."

"I can't help it!" Alfie let the book drop to the floor and continued staggering around the room.

"You had better sit down, Prince Alfred. Here, let me help you." Mrs. Stickler tried to grab Alfie's arm, but he swayed out of her reach and bashed into a tall bookcase, sending books tumbling from the shelves.

"Ouch! I wish I could stop wobbling," he cried, staggering toward a table with a priceless crystal vase.

Bea tried not to laugh. She should never have told her brother to make his distraction something big! She really hoped he didn't break anything. While Natasha and Mrs. Stickler tried to catch hold of Alfie, Bea crept to the door. When she opened it, a furry face peeped through.

Bea shooed the puppy backward and slipped out, closing the door behind her. She tried to scoop the little dog into her arms, but the puppy scampered off down the passageway.

"Hey, wait!" Bea called softly.

The puppy galloped into the drawing room, jumped onto the sofa, and nipped playfully at the cream-colored cushions. Bea inched up to her, but as soon as she got close, the puppy dashed away again. The little dog raced around the dining room, barking excitedly, before running right up the stairs.

Bea rushed after the puppy, who had stopped at the top to sniff the carpet. She crept up the last few steps and pounced!

"Got you!" she whispered into the puppy's soft fur as she ran to her bedroom and closed the door. "We're lucky no one saw us. You're a pretty fast runner, aren't you?"

The puppy licked Bea's cheek.

"How did you escape from the laundry room, anyway?" said Bea. "Did you push the door open? You need to remember that you're a secret. Some people would be upset if they knew you were here."

There was a rustling in the box under the bed, and the puppy's ears pricked up. Bea pulled out Fluff's cardboard box and set it on her chest of drawers, out of reach. The little dog wagged her tail and then lay down, resting her chin on her paws.

Bea stroked her pale coat and her silky soft ears. "Maybe I ought to think of a name for you."

The puppy gave a huge yawn and rolled onto her back, showing off her tummy. Bea grinned as she rubbed the puppy's soft belly, but her smile faded as she wondered what her dad would say. How was she going to keep a puppy secret at Ruby Palace?

Chapter Four
The Secret Way over the Wall

Bea stroked the puppy's soft ears. "What shall I call you? Maybe I could name you Patch because of your patchy coat. Or maybe Rusty. What do you think?"

The dog bounced up again and dashed around the room, sniffing everything. Her little tail wagged eagerly.

Bea wrinkled her forehead. "You're right! Those names are no good. I'll think of something better."

The puppy gave a soft bark and her ears pricked up. A moment later, Bea caught the sound of footsteps. She jumped up, wondering where to hide the little dog, but when the door burst open, it was only Alfie. "It took me ages to get away!" he panted.

Bea pulled her brother inside and quickly shut the door. "Come and see the puppy I found in the fountain. Isn't she cute? I'm just trying to decide what to name her."

"Call her Firestorm!" Alfie crouched down and shook the dog's paw enthusiastically.

"You have to be gentle. She's only a puppy!" Bea dropped to the floor beside her brother. "Anyway, I don't think Firestorm really suits her. I was thinking of calling her Patch, but I'm not sure it's quite right."

"How about Splash? Because you found her in the fountain." Alfie let the puppy lick his hand. "What's that smell?"

"It's the herbs from the garden—the scent must have brushed off on her coat." Bea put her arms around the little dog. "That's it! I can name her after one of the herbs. Rosemary sounds nice—Rosie for short!"

The puppy galloped to and fro before stopping to bark at herself in the mirror. Alfie and Bea laughed.

"So are you going to keep her in your room like Crinkly and Fluff?" asked Alfie.

Bea hesitated. She longed to keep Rosie, but she needed to find out whether someone was missing the little dog. "No, I think I'll take her for a walk and ask

around to see if anyone's lost a puppy.
Somebody must know where she came
from."

"I'll come, too!" Alfie told her.

Bea shook her head. "I've got to get
over the palace wall without Mrs. Stickler
seeing. So I think you'd better stay here."

"That's not fair! I helped you escape
from the parlor, so I should get to take
the puppy for a walk, too! And we'd
better hurry. Natasha is coming to find
you to practice the national song."

Bea scrambled to her feet and picked
up Rosie. "Why didn't you tell me
before? Quick, we've got to go!"

The corridor was empty. Bea raced
down the staircase with Alfie behind
her. Just as they reached the front door,
Mrs. Stickler's voice rang out from the
dining room.

"This table is terribly dusty, Jenny. We have some very important people coming to dinner, and everything has to be perfect. Now, where is Princess Beatrice? That girl is always running off somewhere."

"Quick, Bea—" began Alfie, before Bea clapped a hand over his mouth and pulled him outside.

"I'm trying to leave *secretly*, remember!" she hissed into his ear.

Mrs. Stickler marched into the hallway and looked around suspiciously. Bea watched her, hidden behind the pillar by the front door. She gripped Alfie's arm tightly, warning him not to make a sound.

Once the housekeeper was gone, Bea let go and darted outside. Alfie pulled up his sleeve. "Ow, that hurt!"

"Sorry, but if you're coming along, you have to stay quiet," said Bea.

Rosie ran across the garden, her tail wagging. Bea spotted Mrs. Cherry pulling weeds out of a flower bed and went over to her.

The gardener brushed earth off her hands and smiled at Rosie. "She's such a cute puppy! I haven't found anyone who's missing a dog, though. Do you think she wandered in here by accident?"

"Maybe she came down the road and squeezed under the front gate," said Alfie eagerly. "Or maybe she was left here by a wicked dog snatcher, or maybe—"

"I guess she could have found her own way in," interrupted Bea, before Alfie's imaginings got too wild. "I'll go to the Sleepy Gull Café and ask Keira's mom and dad. Lots of people walk their dogs along the cliff top."

"And I'll ask the rest of the stable hands." Mrs. Cherry tickled Rosie under the chin.

"Thanks, Mrs. Cherry." Bea wondered if it was awful of her to hope that Rosie's owner wasn't found too quickly. She loved having the little dog at the palace!

Alfie and Bea walked into the orchard, the puppy gamboling at their feet. Suddenly Rosie spotted a butterfly and chased it back toward the palace. The puppy was halfway across the orchard when a stripy kitten leapt out from behind a bush with a shrill meow! Tiger tried to pounce on Rosie's tail but missed.

"Be friendly, Tiger!" Bea scooped up the little kitten, who snuggled against her, purring.

Rosie barked up at them both, her tail wagging.

"I think Rosie wants to be friends," said Alfie. Bea set Tiger down on the

ground. The kitten's back stiffened, and
when Rosie tried to run up and sniff
him, he gave a fierce yowl that made the
puppy run and hide behind Bea's legs.
Rosie began to bark over and over.

Bea glanced toward the house. What
if Mrs. Stickler heard? Quickly, she
caught the squirming puppy under the
tummy. Hugging Rosie tightly, she
marched over to a plum tree growing in
the corner of the orchard.

The tree's branches stretched right
over the top of the palace wall. This was
Bea's secret way out of the royal garden.
She patted the knobbly tree trunk. "You
go first, Alfie. Then I can hand Rosie
to you."

Alfie clambered over. Then Bea
climbed up and lowered the puppy into
her brother's hands. "Bye, Tiger. We'll

be back soon!" she called to the kitten
before jumping to the other side.

They followed the path that ran
beside the cliff. The town of Savara was
spread out below them—rows of little
houses with red rooftops. Beyond the
town lay the sea, like a wrinkled blue
blanket dotted with tiny white waves. A
little boat with a snowy sail was gliding
out of the harbor.

Rosie trotted happily beside Bea,
stopping to sniff the air now and then.
The path led past the Sleepy Gull Café
and on toward Shilling Wood. The café
had a cheerful sign above the door and
a large garden with a view of the ocean.

Bea loved the Sleepy Gull Café. The
Makalis cooked the yummiest food
in Savara, and Bea especially loved
their spicy spring rolls. She suddenly

wondered whether Keira and her parents knew about the important people who wanted to come and live on the cliff top close by.

She was opening the gate to the café garden when Rosie's ears pricked up. The puppy's eyes were fixed on a rabbit grazing on the grass. She let out a torrent of barks and hurtled after the creature.

"Rosie," cried Bea. "Come back!"

The puppy sped up, her ears flapping as she ran. The rabbit raced into Shilling Wood, and Rosie chased after it, disappearing under the dark mass of trees.

Chapter Five

The
Sleepy Gull Café

Rosie streaked through the trees, yapping excitedly, and Bea and Alfie rushed after her. The rabbit vanished, and Rosie stopped to sniff a bright yellow orchid. Then she jumped over a fallen log and disappeared into the undergrowth.

"Rosie, wait!" called Bea. "Alfie, did you see where she went?"

"Over there." Alfie pointed to a patch of bushes.

"I should have found a leash for her. She's too little to be running off on her own." Bea wished the fluttering in her stomach would stop. What if they couldn't find Rosie?

She grabbed a stick and used it to push aside the trailing vines. There were paw prints in the mud leading to a tree. Bea followed the marks and discovered a large hole between the roots. Crouching down, she peered into the hollow. "Rosie? Are you down there?"

A furry gray-and-white face poked out. Then Rosie scampered out of the hole, covered in earth and leaves.

Bea brushed the mud off her fluffy coat. "Poor Rosie! I think the rabbit must have gotten away." She picked up the puppy. Tired from all the chasing, Rosie closed her eyes and fell instantly asleep in Bea's arms.

Alfie and Bea left the woods and walked back along the cliff path to the Sleepy Gull Café. The smell of spicy spring rolls drifted out of the café window.

Rosie woke up, her nose twitching. She leapt out of Bea's arms and slipped under the gate into the café garden. Bea sped after her, giggling. Rosie pranced right up to the door and pressed her nose against the glass.

"Rosie, you're so sassy!" Bea scooped up the puppy just as Keira opened the door. Keira had friendly brown eyes, and her long hair was up in a ponytail.

"Hi, Bea." Keira's eyes widened when she saw Rosie. "Where did you get the dog from? Has the king changed his mind about letting you have a pet?"

Bea shook her head. "This is Rosie. I found her in the palace garden, and I'm trying to figure out where she came from. Have you seen her before?"

"I don't think so." Keira tickled Rosie under the chin. "Look at those big brown eyes! I wonder who she belongs to."

Suddenly Rosie jumped out of Bea's arms, darted into the café, and pulled a napkin from an empty table. She galloped back outside with the napkin in her mouth and began digging furiously. Dirt sprayed everywhere as she burrowed with her little paws. Dropping the napkin in the hole, she pushed the earth on top to bury it.

"Rosie!" exclaimed Bea. "Why did you do that?"

"Maybe she thinks the napkin is

treasure!" Alfie's eyes gleamed. "I'll get
another one and see if she buries that,
too." He dashed inside.

Keira giggled. "She's a funny little
thing, isn't she? Can I show her to my
mom and dad? They need cheering up—
we had some bad news this morning."

"What bad news?" asked Bea,
brushing the dirt off Rosie's coat.

"Some rich people want to knock down our café to make room for a big new house." Keira sighed.

"They can't do that, can they?" Bea stared. "It's really unfair!"

"We're going to stop them, so don't worry!" Keira sounded brave, but she chewed her lip as she said it. Then she smiled at Rosie. "Do you think she's hungry? I could see if there's something in the kitchen for her."

Bea called to Rosie and followed her friend inside. Her dad had said his visitors wanted to live on the cliff top, but he hadn't talked about knocking the café down. Bea frowned. Maybe it was all a terrible mix-up.

Keira's mom, Mrs. Makali, was serving customers. She had a flowery apron tied over her skirt, and her black hair was scraped back in a bun. Keira's dad was cooking, and the sound of chopping and sizzling came from the kitchen.

"Hello, Princess Bea." Mrs. Makali glanced at Rosie, who was wagging her tail. "What a cute little dog!"

Bea noticed the trail of dirty paw prints on the floor. "Sorry about the dirt! I'll take her back outside."

Mrs. Makali smiled. "Would you and Prince Alfie like some of my lime-and-coconut cake?"

"Yes, please!" Bea took Rosie to a wooden table in the garden. Alfie dashed to the fence to watch a sailing ship crossing the bay below them.

Keira came out a few minutes later with two slices of cake, a dish of sausages for Rosie, and a brown paper bag that smelled of spices. "My mom wants you to have some spring rolls to take back to Ruby Palace."

"Oh, good! They're my favorite."
Bea watched Rosie munch the sausages
happily.

Alfie bit into his cake. "So what are
we going to do now? I want to show
Rosie to everyone at the palace."

"We can't! Dad will never let us keep
her." Bea frowned at her brother, but
he just shrugged. "Anyway, we haven't
found out who Rosie belongs to. We have
to keep her a secret until we do."

"Fine!" Alfie yawned. "Can we go
back now?"

Bea nodded and took a bite of cake.
She felt a fluttering in her stomach.
She loved the thought of keeping Rosie
at Ruby Palace and playing with her
every day, but how would she make
that work? It wouldn't be easy to hide

a puppy. After all, Rosie seemed to like running off quite a lot!

Alfie and Bea finished their cake, and Bea thanked Mrs. Makali for the spring rolls.

"Bye, Rosie!" Keira knelt down to stroke the puppy.

"I'll ask my dad about those people who want to move here," Bea told her. "Maybe it's all a mistake."

"I hope so!" Keira rubbed her forehead.

"Don't worry!" Bea hugged her friend. "I'll find out as much as I can. We'd better go—there's a fancy dinner tonight, and we can't be late."

Alfie and Bea walked back to Ruby Palace with Rosie scampering ahead of them. Alfie held the spring rolls so that

Bea could carry Rosie back over the wall, and then they crossed the royal garden. Mrs. Cherry, who was digging the vegetable plot, stopped to wave at them.

"I'm hungry! I'm going to find out what's for dinner." Alfie ran inside.

Bea gathered Rosie into her arms again and went to see Mrs. Cherry.

"Hello, Princess Bea." The gardener set down her empty wheelbarrow. "I've got some news about your mystery puppy. I found out where she used to live."

Bea's stomach turned over. Did this mean she'd have to send Rosie back? She would miss the little dog so much! She hugged Rosie tight and tried to smile. "That's great! So where did Rosie come from?"

Chapter Six
The
Wandering Puppy

Rosie wriggled so much that Bea set her
down in the empty wheelbarrow. "I've
been wondering what happened to Rosie
and how she got here in the first place,"
she told Mrs. Cherry.

"Well, she's certainly a long way from
home," said the gardener. "The farmer who
brings the hay for the horses told me about
a stray dog that gave birth to some puppies
in his barn. He thinks Rosie's one of those

pups. She must have crept onto his truck while he was loading the hay and rode all the way here without anyone knowing."

"That makes sense!" cried Bea. "She had some hay stuck to her coat when I first found her." Her stomach lurched as she thought about Rosie all alone on the hay truck. "So, I suppose the farmer wants her back now."

"No, he doesn't. He says he's going to have enough trouble finding homes for the mother and the other pups."

Bea brightened. "Then Rosie will have to stay here! I don't know how I'm going to manage it, but—" She broke off as a shout came from the direction of the palace.

Chef Darou was leaning out of the kitchen window, waving his wooden spoon wildly.

"Oh dear! I was supposed to take Chef

Darou some cucumbers. He must be waiting for them." Mrs. Cherry picked up a sack from the shed and swung it over her shoulder.

"Thanks for finding out about Rosie," said Bea.

The gardener gave her a cheery wave as she headed for the kitchen.

Bea's mind was spinning. So Rosie was a stray after all. It was amazing how she'd made it all the way here on the farmer's truck. The little puppy always seemed to be looking for adventure. If Bea could keep her hidden at the palace, they could have adventures together!

Bea turned back to the wheelbarrow to give Rosie an extra-big cuddle, but it was empty. "Rosie, are you hiding?" She peered under the wheelbarrow. Where was the little dog?

A cold gust of wind blew Bea's hair over her face, and a crow squawked. Its rough cries sounded like a warning. Suddenly the palace garden didn't seem

such a safe place anymore. What if Rosie got stuck in a fountain again? What if she got tangled up in thorny bushes or fell down a foxhole?

Bea tried to ignore the tight feeling in her chest. She ran to the shed and looked inside. Then she searched through the bushes. There was no sign of the puppy.

"Rosie? Where are you?" Bea gazed around the garden. Why hadn't she looked after the puppy better? She should have noticed Rosie running away. There were a million places she could be . . . the orchard, the stables, the maze . . .

The maze was a jumble of twisting and turning hedge walls. If Rosie had disappeared in there, Bea might never find her! She dashed across the garden in a panic.

A long, squeaky howl sounded in the distance. A lump grew in Bea's throat. That *had* to be Rosie. A second howl rose even higher than the first. It was coming from the palace!

Bea raced through the front door, stopping in the hallway to catch her breath. Was Rosie stuck in one of the rooms? Maybe she'd gotten into a really small space and couldn't get out again.

Jenny scurried away from the kitchen, clutching her apron. "I wouldn't go in there, Princess Beatrice. There's an awful fuss, and Mrs. Stickler's in a terrible mood." She curtsied and hurried upstairs.

Bea slipped down the passageway. If Mrs. Stickler had seen Rosie, there would be Big Trouble. She would just have to find a way to explain everything. Taking a deep breath, she stepped into the kitchen.

An empty frying pan lay beside the stove, and the floor was dotted with muddy paw prints. Mrs. Stickler and Chef Darou were standing by an overturned crate. Something was moving underneath it, and a pair of sad brown eyes peered through the wooden slats.

"Who let that little beast into my kitchen?" Chef Darou shook a spatula menacingly. "It's taken a sausage right out of the frying pan, and just look at the state of the floor!"

"It's not just your kitchen. There are dog hairs around the whole palace," snapped Mrs. Stickler. "You should thank me for trapping the creature before it caused even more mess."

Bea's insides went cold as she stared at

the puppy trapped inside the crate. "You can't keep Rosie in there. You're scaring her!" she cried. "Let me take her, and I promise she'll never come in here again."

Mrs. Stickler's stare was colder than an icicle. "Princess Beatrice, do you know something about this creature?"

"Yes, I do!" said Bea. "I found her in the garden this morning. She came all the way here on a hay truck, but the farm doesn't want her back because she's a stray."

"I'm not surprised." Chef Darou wrinkled his nose. "It's a grubby little thing, and it certainly should *not* be in my kitchen."

"It shouldn't be anywhere in the palace!" Mrs. Stickler's eyes flashed. "It's bad enough having that kitten sleeping in the laundry room at night. The king will *never* allow a dog in the palace! The silly animal—rushing around the place like that."

"It's not Rosie's fault!" Bea said quickly. "I was busy talking to Mrs. Cherry, and I didn't notice her jumping out of the wheelbarrow and running away. Just let me take her—please!"

Rosie began to whine. Bea crouched down by the crate and stuck her fingers through the slats, but she couldn't reach the little puppy.

Mrs. Stickler frowned. "*You* shouldn't be in here, either, Princess Beatrice. Princesses are not supposed to wander around the royal kitchen. And I certainly can't let you take this creature away. Goodness knows how many diseases it's carrying."

Chef Darou gave a little shriek, pointing his fork at Rosie. "*Someone* has to take it out of my kitchen. The dinner is supposed to be ready soon, and I still have fish to fry and peppers to stuff and—"

"There you are, Bea!" Natasha marched in. "I've been looking for you for *hours*. We haven't even started practicing the song yet. Don't you want to get it right? We—" She broke off, staring at the crate with Rosie beneath it.

Mrs. Stickler tutted. "Oh dear! Well, you can't practice now—you both need to get changed."

"Is there a dog in there?" Natasha's eyes widened.

"Yes, I found her in the garden this morning." Bea turned to Mrs. Stickler. "Please let me take her. I promise I'll keep her out of the way!"

"Don't you think we should let the dog out?" added Natasha. "What if it gets hungry or thirsty?"

Mrs. Stickler tightened her lips. "I shall move the crate into the corridor and leave a dish of water inside, but the animal *must* stay in the crate. The king will decide what will happen to it."

"But please—" cried Bea.

Mrs. Stickler steered Natasha and Bea out of the room. "Hurry up and get ready, please. Mr. Jennings has delivered your new dresses, and I'm sure you're going to love them. Don't forget, your father wants you looking neat and tidy when you meet Lord and Lady Villiers this evening. Your face needs washing, Princess Beatrice, and your hair needs a really good brushing."

Bea stumbled down the passageway, tears pricking her eyes as Rosie's whines grew into a howl behind her.

Chapter Seven
The Profiterole Prank

The housekeeper followed Bea and Natasha upstairs, talking about hair ribbons and shoes the whole time. Bea shut her bedroom door, thankful when Mrs. Stickler finally went away.

Bea tried to swallow a huge lump in her throat. She would give every single shoe and ribbon she owned to get Rosie back. The little dog just wanted to run around and play. It was so unfair that she was trapped under a crate for acting like any normal puppy.

The new dress was hanging on the outside of the wardrobe. It was orange—Bea's least favorite color—and it was covered with scratchy-looking sequins. Bea put it on and picked out a bright green hair ribbon. Mrs. Stickler would probably say this color clashed horribly with the dress, but she didn't care.

Picking up her hairbrush, she tugged at her tangled hair. There had to be some way to get Rosie out of that crate. Everyone would be busy tonight because of the visitors and the dinner. Maybe they wouldn't notice if Rosie disappeared.

It would be handy if something went wrong at the dinner—like the soup getting spilled. Then everyone would be distracted and no one would be watching the puppy. But what if nothing went wrong at all?

An idea popped into Bea's head, and her face brightened. She would make sure something went wrong! Nothing huge—just a little mistake that would get everyone's attention. Alfie might help her. He was good at disasters.

Bea threw the hairbrush on the bed, opened the door, and came face-to-face with her sister. Natasha was wearing a purple satin dress with a matching ribbon and a shiny pearl necklace. Her hair was so neat, it looked like she'd brushed it a thousand times. "I'm sorry about the dog, Bea, but you really shouldn't have brought it inside. You know what Dad will say."

"Rosie didn't have anyone else to look

after her! I *had* to bring her in," cried Bea.

"I know Dad let the kitten stay, but that was only because the grooms said a cat would be useful for chasing rats away from the stables," Natasha went on. "Dogs are a lot more work, and the palace is no place for a pet!"

Bea scowled. She was fed up with everyone saying that! She stormed past her sister.

"Aren't we going to practice the song now?" called Natasha, but Bea kept walking.

Rosie's crate had been moved into the corridor outside the kitchen. As Bea came closer, the puppy pressed her nose to a gap in the box and barked softly.

"It's all right!" Bea knelt down and

whispered through the wooden slats.
"I've got a plan to get you out of there.
Just hang on . . ." She jumped up as Chef
Darou marched down the passageway,
muttering about squashed tomatoes.

Bea peered into the kitchen. The
maids, Jenny and
Nancy, were rushing
around with dishes
of steaming
vegetables.
A towering
mountain of
profiteroles
stood on an
enormous
silver platter.
The little
cream-filled
pastry balls

were coated with chocolate, and they
looked delicious.

"Princess Beatrice, where are you?"
called Mrs. Stickler. "You'll be late for
dinner."

"Don't worry—I'll be back soon," Bea
whispered to the puppy. She dashed into
the dining room, forgetting all about the
elegant walking that the housekeeper
had taught them that morning.

King George was sitting at the head
of the long dining table with the two
guests seated on either side of him. Crystal
glasses and white china plates shone in the
soft candlelight. Everything was perfectly
arranged, as if Mrs. Stickler had gone
along the table checking the position of
each knife, fork, and spoon with a ruler.

Lady Villiers raised her eyebrows as
Bea hurtled in and sank into a chair

between Alfie and Natasha. The maids brought in the first course, and Mrs. Stickler poured the drinks.

"So have you decided where your new house will be?" King George asked his guests.

Lord Villiers straightened his jacket. "Building a mansion on the cliff top will give us a marvelous view. We visited a possible site a few days ago and decided it was quite suitable."

"That's excellent news!" said King George.

"Yes, we just need to get rid of the drab little café that's already there and the place will be perfect." Lady Villiers picked up her wineglass. Diamond rings sparkled on her fingers.

Bea froze with a forkful of salad halfway to her mouth. "You can't do

that! The Sleepy Gull Café is one of the
most amazing places in the whole of
Savara."

Natasha nudged her. "Bea! Shh!"

"And their spring rolls are yummy,"
added Alfie. "I kept some in my pocket in
case I didn't like dinner." He pulled out
a squashed paper bag and emptied the
spring rolls from Mrs. Makali onto a plate.

Lord and Lady Villiers looked
disgusted, but King George picked one
up thoughtfully. "Yes, they do make
wonderful food up there. It's such a
lovely café."

Lady Villiers sucked her breath in
sharply. "Well! I'm sure you agree that
our mansion is more important than a
silly café."

The king frowned and took a bite of
his spring roll.

After the first course was cleared, the maids brought in the main course—fish pie with carrots and peas. Bea took a forkful of pie, hardly noticing what she was eating. She had to save the café and free Rosie from that horrible crate. She just had no idea how to do it without making all the grown-ups very angry.

"What's the matter with you?" Alfie hissed in her ear.

Bea jumped, flicking a spoonful of fish pie into the air. It landed with a plop in Alfie's lemonade. King George gave them a stern look.

"It's Rosie," Bea whispered back once the grown-ups were talking again. "She ran into the kitchen, and Mrs. Stickler trapped her under a crate."

Natasha leaned over. "I think I can persuade Mrs. Stickler to let the puppy

out. I'll talk to her right after dinner.
Just don't do anything silly . . ."

"Natasha, Beatrice," King George
boomed. "Perhaps after we've had dessert,
you could sing the national song."

"Of course—we'd love to." Natasha
smiled and smoothed her neat hair.

Bea glanced suspiciously at her sister.
She couldn't believe that Natasha really
wanted to help her. Surely that would
be breaking royal rules somehow. Bea
wriggled in her seat while the maids
collected the dinner plates. Time was
running out. She needed to hurry or
Rosie would be trapped under that crate
for the whole night.

When the table was cleared, Jenny
carried in the gigantic silver platter with
its tower of profiteroles. The little balls
of chocolate and cream were balanced

neatly on top of each other. A fluttering feeling grew in Bea's stomach. She knew *exactly* how to make a disaster happen. She jumped to her feet.

"Bea, what are you doing?" hissed Natasha.

Bea walked straight toward Jenny. Pretending to stumble, she bumped into the maid. The silver platter wobbled.

Jenny squeaked as she lost her grip and the tray of dessert flipped over. Profiteroles flew everywhere. They rolled along the table and spun across the floor. One landed on the piano keys with a loud *bong*! Another one bounced off Lord Villiers's face, leaving a chocolaty-brown mark in the middle of his forehead.

Lady Villiers gasped. Alfie grinned. Not a single profiterole was left on the platter. The chocolate balls had spread

everywhere like a swarm of tiny brown creatures.

For a second, no one moved. Then Natasha leapt up with a determined look on her face. "Go now!" she whispered to Bea. "Set the puppy free, and I'll distract them for you." She started handing out napkins and talking loudly about how difficult it was to get rid of chocolate stains.

Bea stared at Natasha in surprise. Her sister really did want to help her! She crept to the door. There was no time to lose. She had to rescue Rosie while no one was watching!

Chapter Eight

A Home
for Rosie

Bea glanced back as she slipped out
of the dining room. Mrs. Stickler was
scolding poor Jenny, who was trying
to gather up profiteroles. Lady Villiers
was dabbing her husband's forehead
with a napkin. Alfie was pretending to
help while stuffing profiteroles into his
mouth.

Bea ran down the corridor, her heart
pounding. Chef Darou was in the kitchen,

muttering to himself as he filled a pot of coffee. Bea knelt down beside Rosie's wooden crate, and her heart sank. The puppy wasn't moving. She wasn't even making a sound.

"Rosie, are you all right?" She peered inside the crate, where Rosie lay curled up, her big, sad eyes blinking. Bea's chest tightened. What if Rosie was ill? It was so mean of Mrs. Stickler to leave her with nothing but a dish of water.

Bea heaved at the crate, struggling to lift it. One side tilted and Rosie squeezed herself out. Bea gathered up the puppy and let go of the crate, which landed with a crash.

Rosie snuffled at Bea's ear and licked her cheek. "Rosie, you're all right!" cried Bea. "I was so worried about you."

"What's going on out there?" called Chef Darou.

Bea hugged Rosie tightly. She had to get away, but where should she go? If she headed to the back door, the chef would see her. If she went to the front entrance, she might run into Mrs. Stickler or her dad. She could go up to her room, but it was the first place everyone would look once they figured out she was gone.

Rosie whined softly and licked her cheek again. Bea tiptoed across the passage and slipped inside the storeroom next door to the laundry room. The shelves were stacked high with bags of flour and rice and boxes of tea. Light from the setting sun shone through the high window.

Bea froze as footsteps passed the door. The window was too high to reach, so she piled up the boxes of tea and climbed onto them with Rosie tucked under her arm. It took a lot of twisting to loosen the latch, but finally the window swung open. Bea scrambled onto the windowsill and dropped down to the grass below.

The fall jolted Rosie and she whimpered, so Bea stroked her gently till she was calm. Suddenly, Bea realized her whole plan had been to free the puppy. What was she supposed to do next? There was no point going back inside. Mrs. Stickler would take Rosie away, and everyone would still be upset about the profiteroles.

She headed for the orchard, carrying Rosie in her arms, but stopped when she heard loud voices. Lady Villiers stormed out the front door, with Lord Villiers following her.

"I can't believe some little café is more important to the king than what we want," she snapped. "How dare he say we can't knock it down!"

"Never mind, my dear." Lord Villiers opened the door to their limousine. "I did think there were too many seagulls up there anyway."

Bea smiled. At least this was one piece of good news! Her dad had saved the café. She would go and tell Keira right away. Holding Rosie tight, she climbed over the palace wall and headed for the cliff path.

The sea was making a soft shushing sound, broken now and then by the seagulls' cries. The sun was slowly sinking, casting a shimmering golden path across the blue-gray water.

Rosie ran along the cliff path, sniffing every flower and stone. She barked at a moth that fluttered into the air and chased the little creature, her tail wagging.

Bea sat on a rock and rested her chin in her hands. If only she could think of a way to keep Rosie at Ruby Palace . . . but her secret puppy wasn't a secret anymore. Her dad would never agree to keeping the little dog. Rosie needed a good home and people who loved her.

Keira came running down the cliff

path with her jump rope. "Bea! What's the matter? I thought you had a special dinner tonight."

Bea smiled. "I came to tell you some good news! My dad won't let your café be knocked down. Those horrible people will have to find somewhere else for their mansion."

"That's great!" Keira beamed. "But why aren't you happy?"

"Mrs. Stickler caught Rosie, and I had to rescue her. But I can't keep her because . . ." A lump grew in Bea's throat. "No one wants a puppy at the palace."

Keira took Bea's hand. "I'm sorry, Bea! Why don't you come to the café, and I'll get us mugs of hot chocolate. My parents are just tidying up."

Rosie scampered ahead as they walked to the Sleepy Gull Café. Mr. Makali was sweeping the floor while Mrs. Makali stood beside the cash register, counting the money. Keira ran inside and told her parents the good news about the café.

"I think it was the spring rolls that did it!" added Bea. "My dad loves them so much. They reminded him how lovely your café is."

"Well, please tell your father we're very grateful and that I'll make him my special spring rolls every day if he likes!" Mr. Makali laughed. "But you look sad, Princess Bea. Is there anything we can do to help?"

Bea sighed. "It's really Rosie that needs the help. She's a stray, and no one wants her! I really wish I could keep her at the palace, but she loves to run around all the time. She's already stolen a sausage from the kitchen."

Mr. Makali bent down to stroke Rosie. "I used to have a dog with a splendid gray-and-white coat just like this when I was a boy."

Keira tugged her dad's sleeve. "I've always wanted a dog, Dad! If Bea can't keep Rosie, can we have her?"

"Keira!" her mom exclaimed. "Your

dad doesn't want an animal to look after. Anyway, what would our customers say?"

Mr. Makali continued stroking Rosie.

"I think they'd like this little dog as much as we do. Look at her, Anita. How can you resist those eyes?"

Rosie looked up at Keira's mom. Then she lifted a paw and put it on Mrs. Makali's knee. Mrs. Makali's face softened. "Oh well, if you both want to keep her, then I don't mind! But I'm not walking her. I have enough to do already."

Keira beamed as she turned back to Bea. "Should we look after Rosie? I promise we'll take great care of her, and you can visit every day."

"That's a brilliant idea!" Bea's eyes shone. "I think she'll love it here, and I can help out by taking her for walks."

Mr. Makali smiled. "I have a big old cushion that would be perfect for her to sleep on. Let me see if I can find it."

Bea gathered Rosie into her arms and hugged her tightly. "Rosie, this is going to be your new home, but I promise to come see you all the time, and we can go play in the woods just like we did this morning."

Rosie woofed and licked her cheek.

Mr. Makali came back with a little red ball. "Look what I found! Perhaps Rosie would like to play in the yard before bedtime."

Bea and Keira played fetch with Rosie on the grass. The puppy scampered up and down, her ears flapping. Seagulls called softly as they settled on their cliff-top nests. The sun sank into the sea, and the sky faded from turquoise to silver-gray.

Chapter Nine

Friends
Forever

Bea tried to sneak outside before
breakfast the following morning, but
Mrs. Stickler marched her into the
dining room, where Natasha and Alfie
were eating. "You *must* have a proper
breakfast, Princess Beatrice. Oh, we've
run out of grapefruit juice—I'll get some
more."

Alfie grinned when the housekeeper
left. "I poured the grapefruit juice into

there." He jerked his head at a potted plant.

Natasha looked horrified. "Alfie!"

"Well, it tastes awful!" Alfie shrugged and turned to Bea. "Where did you go last night? What happened to Rosie?"

"She's going to live at the Sleepy Gull Café with the Makalis," said Bea. "We can go see her whenever we like."

Alfie spread a thick layer of chocolate on his toast. "I told everyone you were washing a profiterole stain off your dress so they didn't go looking for you."

"Thanks!" Bea glanced at Natasha. "And thanks for helping me get away."

Natasha nodded primly. "I'm glad the dog has a suitable home, but I don't think you should pick up a stray animal next time."

Bea bit back a reply. She knew she'd do exactly the same thing all over again, but there was no point telling her sister that. "Was Dad upset about the profiteroles?"

"I don't think so. But Mrs. Stickler got really annoyed and searched the whole palace when she found out Rosie was gone." Alfie glanced at the doorway. "Watch out, here she comes!"

The housekeeper hurried in and set down the juice. Then she brushed the tablecloth with her fingers. "This is ridiculous! I'm still finding dog hairs everywhere." She frowned deeply. "I can't imagine how the creature escaped from under that heavy crate."

"Maybe she was a puppy with the strength of a triceratops," suggested Alfie. "Maybe she broke out when she smelled all the profiteroles. I think profiter-*roll* is a great name for those things because they rolled a lot."

Mrs. Stickler sniffed. "Yes, I'll be trying to fish them out from under the piano for weeks."

"I saw one under the parlor sofa that must have rolled all the way across the hall! I'll show you." Alfie winked at Bea before pulling the housekeeper through the door.

Bea grabbed a piece of toast and slipped outside. She climbed the palace wall and flew up the path to the Sleepy Gull Café.

It was a bright day with little white clouds sailing across the sky. The sea sparkled, and the yellow and orange poppies growing beside the path nodded

their heads. Mrs. Makali opened the window blinds just as Bea reached the café door.

"Good morning, Princess Bea!" Mrs. Makali looked amused. "I wonder what could bring you here so early."

"I came to see Rosie," said Bea, trying to catch her breath. "Did she sleep all right? Did she like her bed? Has she had breakfast this morning?"

"She's eaten three sausages already," replied Mrs. Makali. "I don't think we'll be throwing away leftover food anymore!"

Bea found Rosie lying on her big comfy cushion. The puppy leapt up and jumped around Bea's legs, barking happily. Keira came over and they stroked the puppy together.

"Hello, Rosie. I'm so glad you're

happy here." Bea rubbed the dog's silky coat.

"She's such a good puppy!" said Keira. "She was waiting patiently when I came downstairs this morning. I bet you missed her, though. Do you think the king will ever let you have a real pet?"

"I don't know. But even if I don't get a pet of my own, I'll never give up caring for animals!" Bea's eyes shone. "Looking after Rosie was so much fun."

Rosie barked and licked Bea's hand, before picking up her red ball.

"Aw, look! She wants to play." Keira jumped to her feet. "Let's go out in the yard."

Bea's heart glowed as she followed Rosie and Keira outside. Rosie had been a stray, but now she had a lovely home. Bea was sure there would be more lost animals that needed her help. She might not have perfect royal manners, but she was wonderful as a princess of pets!